The 89th Kitten

The 89th Kitten

by Eleanor Nilsson

illustrated by Linda Arnold
cover illustration by Elizabeth Miles

SCHOLASTIC INC.
New York Toronto London Auckland Sydney

ISBN 0-590-42413-0

Text copyright © 1987 by Eleanor Nilsson. Illustrations copyright © 1987 by Angus & Robertson Publishers. All rights reserved. Published by Scholastic Inc., 730 Broadway, New York, NY 10003, by arrangement with Angus & Robertson Publishers.

12 11 10 9 8 7 6 5 4 3 2   0 1 2 3 4/9

Printed in the U.S.A.   28

First Scholastic printing, November 1989

*To the youngest daughter
of Ellen Greenfield*

CONTENTS

1 THE BLUE LADY

"It's the eighty-ninth kitten," said Sandy. "Isn't she a beauty?" She held up their latest acquisition — a fluffy white cat with the slightest tinge of pink or apricot in its fur. Sandy thought it was easily the most beautiful kitten in Australia.

"Hardly a kitten," said Miss Berry, looking at the spread and length of the marvelous cat, "but certainly beautiful."

Miss Berry had once lived alone. For many years she had lived alone in the house her parents had left her and never thought anything of it — until she retired. Before that she had clicked the picket gate every morning at half past eight and walked to the post office where she had torn out stamps and listened to people and knitted sweaters, mostly blue, in her lunch hour. On weekends and after supper in the summer she had worked in her huge garden, the largest in the neighborhood and next to the park. Every year she dug up her flower garden and started again. Sometimes she bought seeds and bulbs for color, sometimes for smell. White flowers were best for perfume, but blue flowers she loved. She planted forget-me-nots, hyacinths — always blue ones — irises and little blue daisies. She always wore blue — powder blue and light blue, royal blue and navy blue, ice blue and electric blue. Her house had pretty blue shutters and white frothy curtains that blew out in the slightest breeze for her windows were always open, summer and winter, when she was at home.

Sandy lived two blocks away. She left at half past eight, too, and usually she tried to catch up with Miss Berry. She called her "The Blue Lady" to herself. One day she tried

saying "Hello," and the next day she fell into step beside her.

"We're studying frogs," she said. "But I wish it was something nicer. Miss Silverton says everything is nice, but I've always liked furry things best. Linda likes frogs. She sits next to me. But she might just be saying that. She says she hates the feel of fur, but you couldn't, could you?"

Miss Berry didn't say anything, but she smiled so Sandy went on.

"Miss Silverton says I should talk plenty when I'm out of school and I might use up all I have to say," she said. "But it doesn't seem to work."

Miss Berry smiled again and walked briskly to the post office. Sandy had trouble keeping up with her. She walked faster than anyone she knew.

The first few days Miss Berry didn't even turn around when she got to the post office. But after a week or so she turned and called, "Good-bye." One day she even waved. She likes me, thought Sandy.

Sandy missed her when she stopped work.

She was the best listener she had ever managed to find. She was always interested to hear about Linda, the color of the socks she wore, her latest insults, what she said she did on the weekends.

"Have you seen The Blue Lady?" she asked her mother.

"I haven't for awhile. I did see her in Woolworths one day and she certainly did look a blue lady. Is she always miserable like that?"

"I never thought she was miserable," said Sandy. "Just quiet."

So she looked out for her the next day before and after school, even hung on her gate and peered in the windows, but the frothy white curtains were drawn across and she couldn't see in. But the sprinkler was on and the garden tidy.

The truth was that Miss Berry was depressed. She had hated to leave her lovely house when she went to work and thought of it often during the day sitting waiting for her to come back to it. But now that she was in it all the time she felt bored and restless and very lonely. She could feel the loneliness seeping into her from all parts of the garden, especially from the big stone wall at the back of the house.

When she was working, she never seemed to have much time for people on weekends. There had been the washing and ironing to do, a meal or two to cook to help out during the week, the house to clean and the garden to see to. Talking to people was just a nod and a word over the fence as she ran in and out with the washing, or tidied up the hedge clippings. She didn't miss talking to people because there were the people at work. She could share with them her observations on the weather and politics and what was growing in the garden and the trouble with millipedes and snails.

"What you're needing," said her neighbor one day, "is a big dog, to guard the house and keep you company, especially with that park next door."

But Miss Berry had always been rather afraid of dogs and worried by their barking. So she continued to live alone.

2 BLACKBERRY

But one night when she went out in her slippers to put the milk bottles at the gate she heard a most desolate sound coming from the pine tree, just outside the picket fence. It was the tiniest, most miserable "miaow." Miss Berry clicked open the gate and looked up into the branches. And there was the smallest scrap of a kitten she had ever seen, jet black against the navy of the evening sky.

"Puss, puss," she called uncertainly, but the kitten clung on grimly to the twisted trunk. Miss Berry reached up for it but it was too far. She went back for the chair on the verandah and put it under the tree.

"Nice kitty," she called reassuringly. "Dear puss." The kitten appeared to be listening. Certainly it had stopped miaowing.

Miss Berry stepped briskly up onto the chair and put her hands around the little cat. It was so tiny that her fingers seemed to be lapping around one another with nothing in between. She stepped down gently and carried the kitten into the house.

The kitten held itself rigid, then wriggled, then went rigid again. But Miss Berry kept a firm, gentle hold on it and set it down by the fire. The kitten dived under the sofa.

"Black as night, got a fright," said Miss Berry soothingly, crawling around on the floor, trying to get a view of it. Then she thought of heating some milk and setting that on the floor. She found a green plastic bowl and filled it with the warm, creamy milk. Then she sat down with the paper and pretended not to watch as the kitten crept out on its belly and quickly and guiltily, with many little starts and sideways glances, lapped up all the milk. The little pink tongue went around and around the bowl, licking up the splashes that clung to the edges. Then the kitten pawed the bowl around the floor as if it were looking for more milk.

"Poor thing," said Miss Berry. "How thin you are!"

The next day she carefully watched the kitchen clock all the afternoon, and at three o'clock she walked up the street past the post office looking for Sandy. She needed someone to share her happy news with. Sandy's face lit up.

"Is it very small?" she said.

Miss Berry nodded.

"How small? This small?"

"And so thin," said Miss Berry. "Starving. It sat on my slipper this morning when I heated its milk. Last night it hid under the sofa."

Sandy ran ahead, clicked open the picket gate and waited, first on one foot, then on the other.

They found the kitten curled up on the sofa. Sandy sat beside it, then picked it up and put it on her knee. It kept slipping off. She pulled each whisker out gently with her fingers and stroked each tiny paw.

"What will we call it?" she asked.

"Blackie?" suggested Miss Berry.

"Too ordinary," said Sandy. "What about Old Nick or Devil?"

"Oh, no," said Miss Berry hastily.

"Sooty then, or Jet, Ebony, Coal . . ."

But Miss Berry's face still had a waiting look, as if they hadn't hit on the right name yet. Sandy looked at the kitten, then at Miss Berry and back.

"I know," she said. "He's your cat, so his surname is Berry. Call him Blackberry."

"Blackberry," said Miss Berry, stroking him.

The tiny frame of the kitten was suddenly shaken by the most enormous purring.

3 KNOBBLES

Every afternoon after school Sandy called in "to see if Blackberry was growing properly." She brought ribbons for him to play with and a red rubber ball; she made shadow puppets on the wall with her hands and taught him how to chase them.

Miss Berry had given him several balls of wool that were soon wound around all the chair and table legs in intricate patterns, and she had bought him a little cat basket. But although his basket looked so sweet with a bow over the top and a frilly blanket inside, he preferred the chairs or their knees or to sit on Miss Berry's slipper while she watched

the news on TV. Sometimes Sandy would run up to the shop for some cat food or fresh scraps from the butcher or "a nice kidney," as Miss Berry put it. Sandy didn't like asking for that.

"I wonder what happened to the others," said Sandy one day as she fondled the kitten.

"What others?" said Miss Berry.

"Cats never have just one kitten."

Miss Berry said nothing at the time but she brooded about it and unconsciously, when she went out with the milk bottles at night, she was listening for miaows. She took to going for a short walk in the park after supper when the street was quiet and she could listen better.

The first week she heard nothing. But during the second week an elderly tabby with bumps on its head rubbed against her legs. She knelt to pat it, half afraid of what she would find. As she had thought — all ribs. The cat was starving. When she walked back home the cat followed, followed her in through the picket gate, followed her up the path, and miaowed at the shut door of the house.

Miss Berry listened in the hall. She thought of how happy she was, with just Blackberry, and of how this cat might give him some disease. But it had looked so frail and ill in the half light that she opened the door and let it in.

After school the next day Miss Berry and Sandy took Knobbles to the vet.

"That has to be his name," said Sandy. "Because of the knobbly bumps on his head."

Sandy liked going to the vet's. She had sometimes been there with her own cat, Napoleon, and once with the canary, Sunshine, who had suddenly died after a hot spell when her father still lived with them. He had helped her bury the canary underneath the pink flowering plum.

There was a clean smell at the vet's and a pretty garden, and you never knew what pets you would see. Often it was just dogs and cats. But sometimes you would get a bird — a parrot or a cockatoo or even a magpie —

or a lizard or a turtle, and once there was a Kangaroo Island kangaroo. But today it was all German shepherds, except for one other cat, a Siamese.

Miss Berry cradled the old cat in a clean towel with frayed edges in a color that had once been pink. Knobbles's sparse hair clung to his skeleton of a body. His tail hung limp and skinny over her arm. Sandy could see the Siamese owner giving them looks. "Fancy letting that cat get into such a state," the looks seemed to be saying, or perhaps, and even worse, "Fancy bringing a mangy old cat like that to *our* vet."

The vet patted him and felt him all over. He didn't seem to mind the bumps.

"Quite an old cat," he said in his quiet voice. "He'll need a vitamin supplement from now on, possibly hormone tablets, and I'll have to fix up his teeth. Quite an expense," he warned, "and he is, as I said, quite an elderly cat. A stray?"

"Yes," said Miss Berry. "And well worth the fixing." And she patted the bumps on Knobbles's head.

After a week or two of pills and fresh meat Knobbles's coat started to shine.

"He looks almost pretty," said Sandy encouragingly.

He was certainly a friendly cat and nice with Blackberry. They often lay together during the day, if it was cold or wet, on Miss Berry's soft patchwork quilt.

4 THE FIRST HALF DOZEN

But Sandy had to go outside, however cold or wet it was, and she caught a bad cold.

"It's not changing out of your wet things when you get home," scolded her mother.

"My shoes got wet," said Sandy.

"But how can that be? We only got them last month. You'll have to stay home for a few days, and I just can't take time off from work."

"Don't worry," said Sandy. "I'll be fine. I'll watch TV and read."

"I'll get Mrs. Simpson to look in every day at lunch, just to see you're all right."

On her second day home she was half dozing in the living room when the neighbor popped her head in.

"Are you all right? Want anything? There was an accident in the next street this morning. Just the usual. Stopping too quick and cars crashing into the back of one another, like shopping carts in the supermarket. Mrs. Daw's been out shopping again — back with a huge package — blankets this time we think. And Miss Berry was asking for you up at the butcher — out getting meat for her cats, she said, and sure enough when I went past, there they were, all five of them, lined up along the windowsills sunning themselves."

"She only has two," said Sandy. But when Sandy was well enough to go around to Miss Berry's she was amazed at what she found in the kitchen. There were four cats now and two kittens, purring and ready to rub themselves backwards and forwards against her legs.

"Where did they come from?" asked Sandy.

"You'd never think," said Miss Berry seriously, "the cruelty there is in this nice neighborhood. These cats, all wandering around starving, and people with two cars.''

"They're not starving now," said Sandy, watching Miss Berry feed them fresh scraps from shining red, green, and yellow bowls.

Miss Berry had put a grocery carton for each of them in the kitchen. Blackberry seemed to like his — at least he liked visiting it. He jumped in and out of it several times even as Sandy watched. Miss Berry had put Blackberry's name on the side of the carton. Sandy set about thinking up names for the others.

"Shadow," she said. "That's the gray one. Honey for you, Panther for the big black one with the thick feet, and Strawberry for the new kitten. Isn't she gorgeous?"

Miss Berry contentedly wrote the names

on the sides of the cartons with a black felt pen.

"Whether they'll go in the right ones . . ." she said.

"It won't matter," said Sandy. "It's really for us."

"They're eating quite a lot," said Miss Berry. "I'm surprised. I got what I thought would last most of the week, but I'll have to go out shopping again tomorrow." Blackberry was pawing his food all around the kitchen floor in and out between the cartons.

"Perhaps you're giving them too much," said Sandy. "If she's playing with hers she's getting more than she needs."

" 'He,' " said Miss Berry. "I'm sure Blackberry's a 'he.' "

"Miss Berry's got five cats now," Sandy told her mother. She counted them off on her fingers. "Blackberry, Knobbles, Shadow, Honey, Panther, and Strawberry."

"That's six," said her mother. "Oh, dear."

"Why do you say it like that?"

"Well, cats seem to attract cats. Six is more than enough. I hope she won't . . ."

"I think it's nice for her," said Sandy. "You would have to spoil it. She's happy. You said yourself she was miserable."

"There's no need to snap," said her mother. "I am pleased. I just hope she does it in moderation, that's all."

But the next afternoon, at the house with the blue shutters and the big garden, Sandy thought about what her mother had said.

"It worries me," said Miss Berry. "It worries me thinking of all the other cats that aren't getting fed. Starving in the streets, hollow-sided, looking in trash cans, miaowing at closed doors."

"Perhaps you've got them all," said Sandy, feeling uneasy.

"No," said Miss Berry, very definitely, getting up and going to the window. "I haven't got them all. I hear them at night. I dream about them."

5 TOO MANY CATS

That evening, after she had put the milk bottles out, Miss Berry found that her slippered feet were leading her into the park. It was late and very dark and the bushes took on strange shapes and twigs cracked very loudly even under her slippers. She stopped and listened. It was completely still. And then she heard a scratching, scraping noise followed by a loud rattling that made her jump. A shape darted out of a garbage can.

In a shaky voice Miss Berry called to it. "Puss?"

Then, more confidently, "Puss, puss."

The cat appeared from behind a eucalyptus

tree and looked at her. She searched in her apron pocket, but there was nothing there but a few squares of chocolate. She walked toward home, calling now and then, and leaving a trail of chocolate squares behind her. Like Hansel, she thought. She paused at the gate and turned. Green eyes glared at her from the edge of the park. She went inside and came back with a bowl of milk which she put at the door. It lay undisturbed all evening. But in the morning the bowl was dry.

The next night she left two bowls on the porch, one with milk, the other with scraps. And she left the door open. On the third night a shadow glided in during the evening and joined the other cats in the kitchen.

"I'd like to call the new one Chocolate," said Miss Berry.

Sandy was helping feed the kittens.

"But it's tabby, not chocolate at all."

"But it came for chocolate," said Miss Berry as she knelt down to give it a pat. "Or seemed to. And that must be unusual."

Miss Berry found that she was going out

every evening, listening for the miaows of the distressed. She was always relieved when she didn't hear any, yet at the end of a week she had another four cats. Sandy named them Lightning, Sober Sides, Drink of Water, and Creamy Paws.

"And that will be enough," she said to Miss Berry quite sternly. "No more looking for lost miaows. It's getting too expensive and the kitchen floor is almost covered with cartons."

"I know," said Miss Berry in a lost sort of way. "It's just when they fill out and purr and look happy I start to think of all the others outside."

"You didn't think about it before," said Sandy. "Now don't think about it again." The words were really suggested by what her mother had said to her the night before.

"It's getting out of hand," her mother had said. "All those cats. People will start saying she's peculiar and calling in the Council. She was always so proud of her lovely clean house, too. I can't understand it."

"It's still clean," said Sandy indignantly. "She keeps the cats beautiful, too. We brush

them every Saturday and we feed them outside now."

In a few weeks, sure enough, everyone was talking. "Poor Miss Berry is getting eccentric since she retired," the neighbors agreed. "Her house and garden are overrun with cats."

"She always did overdo things," said her nearest neighbor. "Remember how she'd be out cleaning her windows every weekend?"

"That's what I don't understand," said Mrs. Simpson. "Her house is so clean and her garden a picture. She's the last person I would have thought who would have packed it with cats. It'll be a slum."

"No," said Sandy's mother. "No, it isn't. It's as clean as ever. I don't know how she does it, but it is."

"And then again, cats are such wonderfully clean creatures that perhaps it isn't so surprising," added Mrs. Tomley.

"But in such numbers!" said Miss Fairweather. "I counted twenty last week."

"I counted thirty-two yesterday," said Miss Berry's nearest neighbor.

"She'll have to be reported," said old Miss Pike. "She's gone senile. Needs to be protected from herself. And what it must be costing!"

"Oh, she was never short of money," said Mrs. Simpson.

"Fancy her becoming odd," said Miss Fairweather.

"I think she's just kind," said Sandy's mother. But she decided to ask Sandy a few questions when she got home.

"How many cats has she?" asked her mother.

"Some are kittens," said Sandy unhelpfully.

"Yes, but how many altogether?"

"There's Blackberry and Knobbles, Panther, Honey, Strawberry and Shadow, Lightning, Drink of Water, and Cream Puff," said Sandy, trying to think of them in order of acquisition. "Chocolate, Sober Sides, Foam and Pirate, One Sock, Creamy Paws, Suds, and Blue Haze. . . ." Her mother's face was getting longer.

"About how many?" she said.

"Thirty maybe, give or take a few."

"It's take, and more than a few, that's needed," said her mother. "It's just too many cats. Mrs. Simpson and Miss Fairweather are organizing a petition, and really I agree with them."

"You couldn't sign!" said Sandy. "If you sign, I'll never speak to you again. They're well looked after. We do a good job with them. And the yard's clean, and Miss Berry's put a wire fence up to keep them in. It's a big garden."

"Yes, but you need a license to keep as many cats as that. It's not a cats' home. Not an official one, I mean," she said hurriedly, for she could see that Sandy was about to contradict her. "It will give the district a bad name."

That's all she cares about, thought Sandy angrily on and off the next day. But when she got to Miss Berry's after school there were three new cats. Sandy felt suddenly helpless. She couldn't face finding names for them. She remembered how she had felt when she was a small child and no one had told her to stop eating the ice cream in the big container, and she had just gone on and on.

"Two were in a carton at the gate," said Miss Berry placidly. "I'm afraid people are starting to dump them."

But Sandy knew that Miss Berry was still going out every night looking for cats. The thought filled her with alarm. She wondered how she could stop her before finding the cats and making them happy, which was nice, turned into a kind of nightmare.

"Aren't you frightened of the dark?" she asked.

"Not of the dark but of what might be in it," said Miss Berry. "But then I think that part of what might be in it is a hungry cat like Blackberry, and that makes me go on."

"I wish I could come, too," said Sandy wistfully, but she knew that there was no point in even asking her mother if she could.

"I know it can't be much fun coming home to an empty house, Sandy," her mother had said that morning. "But I can't help it. I've got to work. And I know, because now, with all those cats, I'm the one coming home to a house that's empty."

"It isn't empty," said Sandy. "You've got Napoleon."

"And don't always be contradicting," said her mother, angry now instead of sad. "And I want you home no later than five-thirty from now on."

Yet, on the whole, Sandy associated the cats with peace. Whenever she felt upset or even when she didn't, she stole off on the weekends to look at them. Not really to play with them, just to look. They were such peaceful creatures — sleek and well-groomed now — basking in the sun. This Saturday when she went, some of the kittens were playing in the honeysuckle, trailing it out in their paws. Creamy Paws was licking them and Pirate was staring fixedly into the park as usual. Only Mournful kept up the subdued, desolate miaow that he always put on when there were people around.

"You can learn a lot from just looking at cats," Miss Berry had said to her. And it was true. Sandy felt calmer inside just thinking about them. Looking at them she felt completely at peace.

6 VISITING

"Your mother — is she well? I mean, is she all right?"

Sandy pretended not to hear him. She walked around to the other side of the ferry and looked at the zoo appearing now steeply above them. How noisy the ferries were, she thought, and busy. Just like self-important businessmen bustling back and forth to work.

She was spending a week with her father in Sydney. Ferry trips, an Opera House tour, a trip to Manley, a walk around old Sydney, a bus to Bondi Beach — the usual tourist beat with her father as tour guide. She wished she hadn't come. There was nothing to talk to him about now. And she couldn't stand how polite he was. He'd always been a bit bad-tempered, a bit boorish, "at least at home," her mother said, but she'd gotten used to it, found it reassuring. She'd almost liked it, she suddenly realized.

A bus took them to the zoo. They came in the front entrance, through the shop with all its touristy things. Sandy hated them — the toy monkeys on sticks, the mugs, the posters. Why can't people just come and look at the real thing? she thought. They walked down steep, winding paths past enclosures where some of the animals were kept.

Sandy stopped to look at the tigers for a long time. They made her feel sad, for they were restless and not contented, and they reminded her of the cats which filled her with such mixed feelings of peace and trouble and the edge of a nightmare.

The breeze was blowing her father's hair in his eyes and making him look younger. Sandy could almost imagine what he must have looked like when he was young.

"Do you think it's wrong to collect things?" she asked him.

"No, of course not. It's a very great urge. Although of course it would depend on what things, and why. Human skulls, for instance. Butterflies, too, I would say, though some people think it's all right. People will collect anything. Shells after wars. Bits of planes. But most things are good to collect. Do you mean like in the zoo?"

And she found herself telling him about the cats.

They stopped to look at the monkeys in their open enclosure while Sandy talked on. She told him how she was running out of names and she was sure Miss Berry was running out of money as she kept going to the bank for what she called "capital." And yet helplessly, just as if Miss Berry couldn't stop herself, as if she was on automatic — Sandy desperately tried to explain to her father — she went to the park every night after dark looking for more kittens.

They were walking back to the bus that would take them to the ferry. The light was changing and the breeze was getting strong. Soon it would be quite cold.

She waited anxiously to see what her father would say about Miss Berry and the cats. But he said nothing as the bus jolted its way down to the harbor and to the self-important ferry that was already chugging across the water to pick them up. The water was turning from glass blue to pink. She waited for him to say how awful or how queer or what did the neighbors say, or even what did her mother say. But he said none of those things. He just looked thoughtfully out over the water and his voice sounded sad as he said, "She's learned to care too much. She doesn't know how to stop caring."

"Mom says they'll make her stop soon. The neighbors are going to call the Council. They're all signing a petition."

"Yes, of course," he said. "They will. They would. People only want you to care in moderation."

"What does that mean?"

But he didn't answer her.

"Let's think up some extra names for your

cats," he said. "You'll need more after being away for a week. Most people name cats according to their color, I suppose. We don't do that with people."

"I do," said Sandy. "I call Miss Berry 'The Blue Lady.' " But he went on as if he hadn't heard.

"You could name them according to their natures, although that's hard, especially at the beginning, for cats always hold a lot back. You can see it in their eyes. Or not see it. Or according to where you found them perhaps — Park Cat, Greenfield. Or you could call them after something quite different, like the ferries. You can give them soft cats' names like Paddy Paws, or you can give them people's names, or you can call them after cats that have had poems written about them or are mentioned in books — like Jeoffry or Hodge."

That was the most her father had said to her for a long time — perhaps for years. And when he saw her off on the plane: "Call one Jeoffry," he said.

But Sandy was feeling angry again, angry with him and with her brother Sam who hadn't even bothered to come to the plane, although she was sure he could have gotten time off. So she just gave him a little wave without looking at him and walked on her own to the gangway. She didn't look back.

7 "MY FAMILY"

It was a pity that it was the very next week that Miss Silverton asked them to write an essay called "My Family."

Sandy sat looking miserably at the blank sheet in front of her. Usually she liked writing essays and went straight to work. Today she stared around the room, chewed on the end of her pencil, and bit small pieces off the new pink eraser she had bought in Sydney. Linda was busy beside her, one braid in her mouth, audibly sucking it, while her pencil flew neatly over the page.

Eventually Sandy wrote, "My family is

only my mother." The bleak words stared up at her. Then she crossed them out heavily and wrote, "I live in a small family." That wasn't right either. She crossed it out viciously. "My family is split down the middle," she wrote the third time. "My brother goes to boarding school in Sydney and my father lives there, too. He takes me on outings and is very nice to me for short periods. My mother has me for longer periods and is not so nice. But on shorter ones she would be just the same I expect. My mother calls kittens names like White Whiskers, Spots, Patches, Molasses, and Fluffkins, but my father thinks cats shouldn't be called by their appearance any more than we should be."

She tore that up and took a fresh sheet of paper. She put the title and the date at the top, carefully ruled a margin, counted how many lines were on the page and read her neighbor's work. Linda's essay was filled with happy descriptions of picnics and birthdays with aunts and cousins and grandfathers — all very well for her. Sandy stared out of the window for awhile and then

became aware of Miss Silverton behind her. She was on one of her quiet pilgrimages around the room.

"Not like you, Sandy," she said as the bell went, "to be stuck for something to say. Well, never mind, finish it for homework."

"I can't finish it when I haven't even started it," said Sandy.

Miss Silverton stared at her and turned a deep pink. But she said nothing — just went a bit icy for the rest of the afternoon. She didn't thaw out the next day either when Sandy pulled out her essay, already crumpled, from her bag. "My family is very nice," she had written.

"Sandra," said Miss Silverton, "you are being impertinent. Whatever's gotten into you? You'll sit here at lunchtime until you've written a reasonable essay. Look at Linda's — three pages, and Robert's and Paul's."

Sandy knew she would cry if she said anything at all. She looked down at her book. The world seemed suddenly full of smug children with happy homes and a full complement of parents and children and herself the only one different.

At lunch she wrote an essay about the cats.

"My family is my business," she wrote at the top of the page, then crossed it out lightly. "I can't seem to write about my family," she wrote, more politely, "but I will tell you about our cats." She put in a lot of detail about them and made a list of all their names for good measure. And wisely, Miss Silverton, reading through the crossing out, didn't pursue the matter further.

8 THE COUNCIL

"I think we'll have to start feeding the cats at half past four, Miss Berry," said Sandy one Saturday morning. "It's taking longer now, and Mom doesn't like me getting home late."

That was putting it mildly. She had had a big fight with her mother the night before — all about how she cared more for the cats than she did for her own home. "Some home!" said Sandy, slamming the kitchen door and going off to bed but grabbing another piece of cake sensibly on the way. "Some home with only one other person in it!"

She could see that her mother was on the verge of tears, but she didn't want to see. She should have cried before. She should have shown her father that she'd wanted him to stay instead of being so quiet and well-bred about it.

"Well, if that's what you feel you want, Harry," she had said, "I won't stand in your way."

She should have stood in his way. She should have locked him in the closet, nailed him to the door, strung him from the ceiling with the onions — anything to keep them as a proper family, the four of them together, not the ghost of a family that they had become.

And it must be the same for them, she thought with a shock. Only the two of them and Sam at boarding school most of the time.

"Yes, Sandy, half past four if you like," Miss Berry was saying, puttering around with the cats' bowls. Her eyes were looking a bit glassy these days, Sandy thought, and everything seemed to be taking her longer. She'd noticed, too, that the curtains didn't look so white and billowy any more and there were no flowers, blue or white, coming up in the flowerbeds.

"I think," said Sandy, "we'll have to stop all this feeding them out of bowls. It takes too long and there's too much washing up after. I think we should put their food out on the concrete. If we hose it right away it won't stain."

"But that would be dreadful," said Miss Berry, quite shocked. "It would be treating them as a mass, not as individuals at all."

"Well that's what it's coming to," said Sandy grimly. "If you will keep looking for more cats and taking the ones that people bring, we've got to treat them like that. Do you know you've got over eighty?"

"You've always said 'we' before," said Miss Berry dully.

" 'We'?" said Sandy. "What do you mean?"

"You said, 'You've got over eighty.' And you haven't named the last three kittens yet."

"Cats," corrected Sandy. "I'm running out of names," she said listlessly, "and you must be running out of money, and the neighbors are running out of patience."

Blackberry, Strawberry, and Honey were resting in their cartons. A new kitten, Snowdrop, was trying to climb up the curtains but kept tumbling in a little circle onto the tiles and then unfolding and trying again. But most of the cats were out playing or sleeping in the garden, except Pirate, of course, who was hanging on the fence and glaring out as usual into the park. He seemed to be watching a small girl wheeling her baby carriage full of stuffed animals. Or perhaps he was looking at the man in the green

uniform with the badge on his pocket who
was walking around the fence and looking
in at all angles.

There was a loud ring at the door. Miss
Berry moved slowly from the kitchen with a
bowl still in her hand. It was the man from
the Council. He looked solemnly at Miss
Berry.

"You're not allowed to keep so many
animals in this district," he said. "You'll
need to get rid of these cats. Most of them

anyway. I counted over fifty. The neighbors say eighty. Some inside, perhaps?" Miss Berry didn't say anything.

"Well, I don't need to see," the man said. "You know yourself there's too many. I'll arrange it for you if you like. Just needs a phone call to the Animal Welfare people and they'll pick them up."

Miss Berry spoke for the first time. "And then?" she asked faintly.

"They try to find homes first, and if they can't — it's kinder really, isn't it?"

"Kinder?" asked Miss Berry, looking all around at her beautiful cats. Cream Puff was in the honeysuckle and Foam was chasing butterflies in the clear fresh light. Midnight and Butternut were lying on their backs, soaking in the sun, and Pirate was hanging grimly to the fence. Smoky was checking the cement for traces of breakfast not hosed away and an unnamed kitty was catching drips at the garden tap.

The man from the Council was impatient to be off. He edged toward the gate.

"And how many may I keep?" Miss Berry called after him.

"You can keep up to a certain number without a special license," he said.

"Fifty?" asked Miss Berry hopefully.

"Oh, no, nothing like that. Nowhere near that."

"Thirty?" Miss Berry asked, less hopefully.

The man from the Council couldn't remember, but his gaze happened to fall on the number on the gate.

"Maybe up to twenty," he said, "since you've so much space and I can see they're well looked after and you've got the fencing. So long as there are no more complaints," he added as he got thankfully into his car.

9 SANDY'S PLAN

And that was the day that the Eighty-ninth Kitten came to stay. She miaowed on the doorstep before lunch and then walked in with the greatest of confidence. Miss Berry made a special fuss over her, for she knew it was the last, and Sandy couldn't help but do the same. She was so beautiful, and besides, this time it wasn't even Miss Berry's fault.

The Eighty-ninth Kitten, looking like a fluffy white cloud at sunrise, lay purring on the furry rug in front of the fireplace. "She found the choice spot, too," Sandy said.

"Usually Knobbles and Blackberry share that."

Sandy and Miss Berry sat in the living room with her while they thought about what the man from the Council had said. And as they talked, more and more of the cats walked gracefully in as if they wanted to attend the conference, too.

"We have eighty-nine cats," said Sandy, "and you're allowed twenty. The difference is sixty-nine."

"What will we do?" asked Miss Berry, looking around in despair at all her happy cats.

"We need to find sixty-nine good homes, that's what."

"But how?"

"We'll advertise in the paper," said Sandy. "In the 'Kids Column,' and in 'What's on this Weekend.' We could make it sound like an outing. And ask for black borders around the ads — people will notice then."

"But which sixty-nine?" asked Miss Berry, looking desperate. "And how will we find sixty-nine good people to care for them?"

"Sixty-nine's nothing," said Sandy. "Not if you advertise your product."

"I couldn't part with Blackberry," said Miss Berry, "because he was the first. And I couldn't part with the Eighty-ninth Kitten for she is the last and sounds like a street in New York. Nor with Knobbles or Strawberry or Blue Haze or Suds or Lightning or White Whiskers or One Sock."

She searched for a cat or a kitten that she felt she could part with. There were a few that kept to themselves, like Midnight and Honey and Pirate and Foam. But she liked that — she liked them independent, too. For that was what cats really should be like.

Sandy looked around too and felt sad, but somewhere inside she was relieved. And she tried to sound positive for Miss Berry's sake.

"It's not as though they'll be miserable," she said. "Look at Pirate. He's sick of being cooped up. Since you put the fence up all he's done is hang on it every day. He'd be happier somewhere else. And if we don't the Council will . . ."

"Don't," said Miss Berry. "You're right,

55

Sandy. I'm grateful. Perhaps you could help me word the ads."

"I'll need time to think," said Sandy, going outside and settling down with the cats.

Most were having their late morning nap. Some were giving a lazy, occasional lick to a paw. All looked contented except for Pirate who was clinging to the wire.

"Why don't you relax?" she called to him, and she patted the ground beside her.

But Pirate looked down disdainfully and stayed where he was.

"Sixty-nine cats and kittens free to good homes," Sandy wrote. "Call at 20 Lorikeet Drive, Grenton, Saturday, October 24th, all day." That would do for the "Kids Column." Now for "What's on this Weekend."

"Open House," Sandy wrote. "Cats and kittens. Beautiful, different cats and kittens. Choose from a wide range of beautiful and different kittens and cats, free, but only to good people. All day Saturday, October 24th, 20 Lorikeet Drive, Grenton."

She showed the notices to Miss Berry.

"How will we know they are good people and good homes?" asked Miss Berry, twisting her hands together.

"We've no choice," said Sandy. "We just have to trust them. We could get them to sign something — that we could visit the cats and they could send us a photograph at the end of a year so we'd know they were all right."

"Yes," said Miss Berry doubtfully. "I don't know that people would altogether like that."

"Cat lovers wouldn't mind," said Sandy confidently, "and we don't want the others."

So Miss Berry sent in the notices on Monday morning for Friday's and Saturday's paper. And Sandy spent every afternoon after school brushing the cats and helping Miss Berry get the garden shipshape. Miss Berry cut the grass on Tuesday and Sandy did the edging. Afterwards they put the butterfly sprinklers on full. They hosed down the concrete while the cats watched at a safe distance. Sandy had brought a stiff scrubbing brush out of her mother's box of equipment for cleaning houses, and she scrubbed loose any bits of old food that were stuck.

Miss Berry washed all her white curtains and cleaned the blue shutters. She bought seedlings of white and mauve alyssum and put red geraniums in pots at the door and on the windowsills. On Wednesday Sandy went to Woolworths and got satin ribbons in several colors to set off the varied beauty of the sixty-nine cats and kittens. She came back with packets and packets of mixed balloons as well that she'd bought with her pocket money.

"It'll make it festive," she said, "like a show or a party. It makes people relax more to see balloons. One free balloon with every kitten and two with every cat."

"No," said Miss Berry, "one for each. I'm not having them think less of my beautiful cats."

"It'd be nice to have a drink stand," said Sandy dreamily. "It might be a hot day. And candy and ice cream."

Miss Berry looked alarmed.

"No, Sandy. We'll put cans of soda in the refrigerator. But that's all we can manage.

Oh, and cookies. I'll get extra cookies for the children." She started writing a shopping list. "What do children drink? Lemonade?"

"Yes, and ginger ale, orangeade, things like that. Get all different kinds. And bottles — you get your money back on those." On Thursday Sandy asked Miss Silverton if she would help her make a big sign.

"For our open house," she explained. "For giving away the cats I told you about."

So Miss Silverton found her a large piece of cardboard and penciled in the letters for her.

"I'd do it in red," she suggested, "for easy viewing."

But during the afternoon Sandy began to feel uneasy. What if nobody came? Who would read the notices? Perhaps it would rain and nobody would want to go out. She needed something else. And then she thought of her father. He understood about advertising.

She called his work number. She wanted to phone before her mother got home. She had often seen it here, penciled into the front of the phone book, but had never thought she'd call it, ever. She was expecting him to be annoyed, so she got her defensive voice ready. But she didn't need it. He was pleased.

"Sandy!" he said, sounding really happy. Then anxious. "Is something wrong?"

"No, Dad, of course not. But it's the cats. We have to find homes for sixty-nine. The Council says we can keep twenty. We're having open house this weekend. We've put ads in the paper — can you think of anything else?"

"Television," he said. "That reaches most people. Call Channel Nine." He paused. "But not until tomorrow. Give your name and address first and say you have a human interest story for them. They just might come around if they're short of news.

"Twenty," he said. "You can still manage with twenty, you and your Blue Lady. Keep my cat Jeoffry, won't you?"

Sandy put the receiver down and looked around the room. It suddenly seemed very empty, very dead. He remembered about her calling Miss Berry "The Blue Lady." He was pleased about the twenty. And she hadn't called any of the cats "Jeoffry." But why did he want her to wait until tomorrow before she called? They were running out of time as it was.

But she did wait. The next day she phoned Channel Nine. She gave her name and address first, carefully spelling out her surname, then she said, "I've got a human interest story for you. There's this lovely old lady who is too kind and she's collected more cats than she's allowed, and so we have to find homes for them or the lady and the cats will be very unhappy. The cats will be more than unhappy," she added. "The cats will be dead."

At first the voice at the other end sounded impatient, but as she went on the voice seemed more, if reluctantly, interested.

"Greenfield, you said your name was. Ah yes, Greenfield. We'll come around this afternoon, after four," said the television station. "To number twenty."

Miss Berry was horrified.

"Television crews?" she said. "With cameras? Here? Oh, I think they must have been joking, Sandy. They wouldn't consider our little problem news."

"It is," said Sandy, a bit put out. "It's human interest. They have lots of items like that now, to keep people's minds off wars and violence and car accidents and things."

At three o'clock Miss Berry thought she would change, just in case. She came downstairs in her favorite suit, light blue with a frilly cream blouse. She wore high-heeled shoes in the same blue.

"You look nice," said Sandy, panting in after school. But she had no intention of changing. Her best clothes and her ordinary clothes were the same anyway — blue jeans and a checked shirt, a windbreaker and sneakers.

"I forgot to say," she said, "that that second to last cat, the one who likes to drink at the leaky tap — his name is Jeoffry."

"That is different from the others," said Miss Berry. "Perhaps he's one we could keep."

★ ★ ★

62

Just after four o'clock Channel Nine arrived as promised and took a picture of Miss Berry in her spotless blue tiled kitchen with its white curtains billowing out of the open window. She was cuddling Knobbles, Blackberry, and Creamy Paws. She couldn't find the Eighty-ninth Kitten in time. She tried to talk to the camera about how she had found Blackberry in the pine tree outside, and how it had all led on from that, but she kept talking to the cameraman at the side of the camera and her voice was rather faint and frightened.

The camera then followed Sandy outside where she was beginning the evening feeding. She chatted away quite comfortably as she filled the shining colored bowls with fresh scraps from Mr. Holly's up the road. They had restored the bowls to make it nicer for the cameras.

"It's hard to say," she said, "just how many cats is enough. These are all beautifully looked after, and they would have starved. If you start caring, it's hard to know where to stop."

She paused as a cat rubbed against her hand on its way to chase drips at the garden tap.

Sandy's mother let her stay later at Miss Berry's that night so they could watch the news together. They were the last item, before the weather.

"Doesn't the house look nice?" said Miss Berry, admiring it afresh on the screen.

"And have you ever seen better looked after cats?" asked Sandy proudly.

The camera rotated around, finding Pirate on the fence with Midnight and Butternut looking up at him, One Sock pawing Lightning's dinner, and the kittens chasing one another in the corner by the honeysuckle. Finally the camera gave a close-up of Sandy's beaming face and focused on the big sign with the clear red lettering that Miss Silverton and Sandy had filled in together.

"That'll do it," said Sandy with satisfaction. "It's sure to do it."

"I think you're right," said Miss Berry sadly, patting Creamy Paws and looking around for the Eighty-ninth Kitten. She found her later in the living room where she was pulling threads out of the sofa, with her head cocked prettily on the side.

"We'd better make a list," she said.

10 OPEN HOUSE

Sandy was up at six on Saturday morning, hanging out of the window, guessing at the weather. It was cloudy, but the clouds were wispy and gentle looking, and the blue of the sky was deepening. A real Blue Lady day, thought Sandy. It would be hot by noon. Sandy wondered again if they would have enough drinks for the children. The next moment she wondered if anyone would come.

She had a quick shower and washed her hair, put on her newest jeans and her green-checked shirt, swirled some puffed wheat into a bowl of milk and poured a glass of orange juice right up to the brim and over. Her mother was still in bed when she'd finished.

"I'm off, Mom," she called in at the door.

"Mmm?" said her mother, trying to come to.

"Open House, remember? I'm off to Miss Berry's."

"I'll come later," called her mother into her pillow.

Sandy took her bike — she didn't need it, just to go two blocks, but she could imagine a line of cars already waiting impatiently at number twenty. And she still had to hide their chosen cats: Blackberry and Knobbles, the Eighty-ninth Kitten and Creamy Paws, One Sock and Jeoffry, Strawberry and Blue Haze, Suds, Lightning, Panther, White Whiskers, Drink of Water, Butternut, Shadow, Midnight, Sad Tail, Honey, Tiger and Foam.

But the street was quite empty. Miss Berry was up, washing the kitchen floor. The bags of balloons were spread out waiting on the kitchen table, and the ribbons were ready to be cut.

"Sandy," said Miss Berry, straightening with her hands to her back, "I found the black pen. I thought perhaps you could put names on the ribbons. People like things better if they have names and I'm sure Pirate and Patches at least will be upset if they're called anything else."

"Right," said Sandy, and she started sorting out the ribbons into colors. "Blue or red for the white cats, green for the orange, yellow or blue for the gray, orange for tabby

and white or red for the black?" she suggested.

"That sounds right," said Miss Berry, although really she hadn't heard. "I'll get changed now. Do you think my hair looks tidy? Perhaps I should have had it cut?"

"It's fine. You look fine," said Sandy without looking up from cutting the ribbons. "And no one's coming to choose you."

Miss Berry went upstairs and looked out of her window. "Go outside, Sandy," she

called, "and look up at the chimney."

Sandy raced outside. Fastened to the chimney was Miss Berry's largest white tablecloth. As she watched it unfurled in the breeze.

"FINE CATS FOR FINE HOMES," the tablecloth proclaimed in red felt lettering.

With a big sign and a banner no one would be able to miss them.

By eight o'clock Sandy had put names on the ribbons and tied them neatly, with a big bow, around the necks of all the cats and kittens — all except Pirate. He twisted on the fence and hissed and even scratched Sandy's hand. The scratch rose up in a red, puffy welt. Sandy dabbed at it with a tissue.

"That's not much of an advertisement," she said sternly to him. "If people come and see a scratch like that they'll think you're all wild cats."

But there was nothing wild-looking about the other cats. They were having their morning walk and play.

Some of the older cats were arranging themselves for sleep in sunny places. Knobbles was already snoring on the roof of the shed. The Eighty-ninth Kitten was climbing up the honeysuckle which spread all over the back wall and Blackberry was making dives at the end of his tail. Foam and Suds were pretending to have a fight. Their backs were arched and they were trying to hiss.

It was a quarter to nine when the first car pulled up. It was a blue station wagon spilling over with tiny blond excited children on very thin tanned legs. The children came running over to the gate and crashed through it. Pirate hissed. A worried-looking blonde woman followed them.

"Is this . . .?" she began.

Then she saw the flag and Miss Silverton's big sign and the cats all waiting in a festive manner. Balloons decorated the length of the verandah.

"I want a blue one," said the youngest.

"I want a red one," said the next smallest.

"I want a kitten," said the biggest. "That one," and he pointed to Blackberry.

Sandy had forgotten to put their twenty cats away.

"Oh, I am sorry," said Miss Berry hastily, "but that is my own cat."

"That one, then," said the eldest boy, pointing this time to Panther.

"Oh, dear," said Miss Berry again, looking very flustered, "I'm afraid that, too . . . If you'll just give us a moment Sandy will sort out the cats. Do come in. Will you have a cup of tea and something cool for the children?"

"No, thank you," said their mother. "We're in rather a hurry. I'm taking the boys to soccer practice. Perhaps we could just look around for another one."

Sandy was hastily carrying armfuls of cats and kittens out of the garden and locking them upstairs in the bedroom. Knobbles wouldn't come down from the roof, but Sandy decided to leave him. He should be fairly safe.

"I want the black and white one," said the second smallest.

"That's Patches," said Miss Berry, relieved. "Yes, he's a beautiful kitten. Playful and affectionate."

"Let's take him, Mom," said the eldest boy, anxious to get away.

"I want an orange one," said the youngest.

"Next time," said the mother quickly. "You hold him, dear. He's a lovely one. And small. Patches."

"Do you have something to put him in?" asked Miss Berry. "I got lots of cartons from the supermarket."

"That'd be nice," said the mother, and Sandy rushed inside for one. She cut a little hole out of the top, wrote "Patches" on the side, and brought out the tape to seal the carton up again. She took the kitten from the youngest child. It was dangling rather sadly from his arms.

"I'll take the ribbon off in case she hurts herself with it in the carton," Sandy said.

"I want the ribbon," whined the child.

Sandy thrust it at him.

"And would you mind signing the book," said Miss Berry, "with where you live."

"Sure," said the woman quite nicely. "Would you like me to call and tell you how he settles in? It is a 'he', isn't it?"

"We don't know," said Miss Berry, "not with the kittens."

The car roared off, full of soccer players and Patches. The picket gate shook on its hinges.

Sandy wrote "Patches" in her book, and felt miserable.

"I feel like having something to drink," said Sandy.

"So do I," said Miss Berry, sinking into a chair with Cream Puff. "This will be too much altogether. The whole day. Put the kettle on, Sandy."

But the kettle hadn't even boiled before three cars pulled up outside and three more behind them. The picket gate opened and shut, opened and shut, until there seemed to be grown-ups and children everywhere. Pirate couldn't even make himself heard above the noise.

"Please don't shout," shouted Miss Berry, "or you'll frighten our cats."

Sandy thought that the grown-ups fussed the most. Most of the children seemed to head straight for a cat or more usually a kitten and then stayed with their choice, but some of the mothers especially fussed from one cat to the next.

"That woman in green must have picked up every cat we've got in the place except Pirate," said Miss Berry, quite cross.

"She probably likes them all — just like you," said Sandy.

But then everyone seemed to leave at once — they all rushed down the path as if they were being sucked down it. Sandy had checked that they all signed for their cats and Miss Berry had supplied the thoughtless ones with cartons.

"Make sure the ribbons are off," Sandy called after them anxiously.

A short lull followed. Miss Berry had her cup of tea while Sandy checked the cats and kittens hidden upstairs. They weren't pleased at being locked inside. Some had resigned themselves, like Creamy Paws and Lightning, and were sleeping on the bed. Others, like Foam and Suds, were sitting in a fidgety way in the open window, while Panther and Shadow and even Strawberry were scratching at the door. Blackberry was trying to get into the closet, perhaps thinking that the door would lead him outside.

The cats in the garden were mainly washing themselves as a way of recovering from being fondled and put back. Pirate was even higher up the fence and was miaowing in a despairing sort of way.

"You'd better come down, Pirate," Sandy called. "No one will even see you up there."

By lunchtime thirty-five cats and kittens had gone.

"More than half," said Sandy triumphantly. "Thirty-four to go. But nobody's come at all in the last half-hour. Oh, there's Mom," she said, running to the door to tell her their news.

"Thirty-five! Goodness!" said her mother. "Then you won't need any cheering up. Perhaps you can have these as a celebration. I've made muffins for Miss Berry and chocolate cake for you."

"That is kind," said Miss Berry. "Sit down and have a cup of tea with us."

"And can I interest you in this beautiful

tabby cat?" said Sandy. "Healthy and quite without fleas."

"You certainly do a lovely job with them, both of you," said Sandy's mother, glancing around at the happy cats that were left. "And your house is like a new pin. I don't know how you do it."

"I couldn't have, without Sandy," said Miss Berry. "But it was getting a little difficult even so."

Sandy hadn't heard her say anything like that before.

"It's been a shame, though, about the trouble," said Mrs. Greenfield, picking her way delicately through words as though they were sharp knives. "The Council, I mean, the petition."

"Well," said Miss Berry, "people don't really understand when they see it from the outside. Sandy understood."

"Perhaps you could introduce me to the cats who are left, Sandy," said her mother, "before the afternoon cars start to come. The lull will be because it's lunch."

And she was right. After she went home

at a quarter to two there was a steady stream of cars. Interestingly the later comers seemed just as pleased with the cat choices left to them as the first people had been. "What a beautiful cat!" was a common remark. One elderly lady even took two, Cream Puff and Chocolate. There weren't any kittens left by now.

"Fancy anyone leaving that lovely short-haired gray tabby with the white feet!" cried the last comer of all.

"That's Perfect Puss!" said Miss Berry proudly. "Isn't she lovely?"

11 THE EIGHTY-
NINTH KITTEN

Nobody came after five o'clock, but only
Pirate was left, still clinging to the wire, and
of course Knobbles, who was meant to be
left anyway. Pirate was very high up on the
fence now. He came down gradually as the
sun sank and the dusk began to fall.

"I'm glad no one took him," said Miss
Berry. "I like an independent cat."

"Maybe you could let him out sometimes
for a walk in the park now that there are
only twenty. Twenty-one," Sandy corrected
herself.

But there were only twenty. When Sandy
let the cats out from upstairs there were only

eighteen. The Eighty-ninth Kitten was missing.

"I must have forgotten her," said Sandy miserably. "Or else she slipped out the door when I was checking them. Someone must have taken her."

But they could find no record of her in the book.

"Perhaps someone just took her without saying," said Miss Berry.

Sandy went home for dinner, feeling rather lost, feeling flat.

"Ask your mother if you can come and have dinner with me tomorrow night," Miss Berry called after her.

"Well, dear?" said her mother. "Did enough people come?"

"Yes, they've all gone," said Sandy in a depressed voice. "Except Pirate. But I must have made a mistake about the Eighty-ninth Kitten. We can't find her anywhere."

"Was she special?"

"She was the last one," said Sandy. "She's beautiful. Different. White with just a trace of pink. Like a sail at sunset in Sydney Harbor."

"Oh, your father called," said her mother. "When we were having lunch with Miss Berry it must have been. Mrs. Simpson answered it — she said it rang and rang. He said he'd call back later. That'll be him now. You answer it. It was for you."

She could hear Sandy's high voice talking to her father.

"It went fine, really well. We could have found homes for them all. We kept twenty. Yes, we kept your cat Jeoffry. The TV was great. Great idea, Dad. I'm sure it did the trick. Lots of people said they'd seen it. Yes, the TV men were good. They took lovely shots of the cats and the house. Yes, I'm fine."

And although he hadn't asked, she added, "And Mom's fine, too. She's well. I mean, she's all right."

"Good-bye then, Sandra," said her father's voice, as it faded back to Sydney, back over the harbor, back to the sunset over the harbor.

"Did your father sound . . . ?"

"All right?" said Sandy, but she was smiling as she said it. "Yes, he sounds fine, well, all right."

"Why did you say it in three ways?" asked her mother, pausing with her cup of tea raised.

"Because I'm never sure which one you both mean."

"Sandy," said her mother. "About these kittens, cats. Perhaps we could have one, even two? After all, Napoleon's getting to be an old cat now. I liked that orangey one, Honey, and Shadow."

"You don't need to overdo it, Mom," said Sandy. "But I don't know anyway. Maybe it wouldn't be fair to Napoleon. But I'll ask Miss Berry tomorrow."

"So Mom says we can have one, or even two."

"If you really want to, Sandy, I couldn't say no to you, although I couldn't part with Blackberry or Knobbles," said Miss Berry. "You know, it's strange, but I don't feel able to let any more go, not to anyone else, I mean," she added hastily.

"And not even to me," said Sandy. "That's all right, I know how you feel. And I'd rather think of them here all happy together."

Miss Berry had surrounded herself with her remaining cats. They were all inside except Pirate who wouldn't come in. Creamy Paws sat at her feet, Blackberry was purring loudly on the furry rug, Knobbles was stretching slowly, Strawberry was smiling, and Jeoffry was sharpening his claws. Suds and Foam were thinking about having a fight, and Midnight and Butternut seemed to be waiting for the television to come on. Drink of Water was sitting under the table waiting for scraps to fall, and One Sock, Blue Haze, Panther, Honey, Sad Tail, White Whiskers, Lightning, and Tiger were curled up in the most comfortable chairs. Shadow was sitting in the window, listening to something. And then Miss Berry heard what he heard, too.

"Do you know," she said, unbelieving, "I think I hear something."

They both listened. The cats stopped what they were doing or not doing and listened, too. And then it came again. A lost and sad, a desolate sound, a sound that Miss Berry could never resist.

"I think it's a kitten in the pine tree outside," said Miss Berry, wondering if it could all be about to happen again. Sandy crept worriedly to the door, listened and opened it very slowly. And there on the mat sat a cat. A beautiful cat. A beautiful white cat with just a tinge of pink or apricot. Like sails at sunset, or clouds at dawn.

"It *is* a cat then," called Miss Berry, wondering at the silence.

"A special one," said Sandy, bringing her in.

"The Eighty-ninth Kitten!" exclaimed Miss Berry. "How sensible. She's just been waiting for everything to get quiet."

The Eighty-ninth Kitten jumped down, her fur standing up everywhere, and licked herself all over in a disdainful and proud way. Then she walked over to the furry rug and nudged Blackberry and Knobbles off it.

"It's twenty-one," said Sandy. "What will the Council say?"

But the Council never came back to check.